BUDDY ROCK'S RACE

For Raphael – K.G.

———

For Mary – S.M.

Text Copyright © 1992 by Kate Green
Illustrations Copyright © 1992 by Steve Mark
Published by The Child's World, Inc.
123 South Broad Street, Mankato, Minnesota 56001
All Rights Reserved. No form of this book may be
reproduced or transmitted in any form or by any means,
electronic or mechanical, including photocopying,
recording, or by an information storage and retrieval system
without express permission in writing from the publisher.
Printed in the United States of America.

Distributed to schools and libraries
in the United States by
ENCYCLOPAEDIA BRITANNICA EDUCATIONAL CORP.
310 South Michigan, Ave.
Chicago, Illinois 60604

Library of Congress Cataloging-in-Publication Data

Green, Kate,
    Buddy Rock's Race: letting go: a fossil family tale / story by Kate Green; illustrated by
Steve Mark.
        p. cm.
        Summary: When Buddy Rocks trips among the other dinosaur runners and comes in
last in the race, his father gives him advice on letting go of his feelings of anger and
frustration and moving on to new challenges.
        ISBN 0-89565-781-3
        [1. Winning and losing – Fiction.   2. Failure (Psychology) – Fiction.   3. Sucess –
Fiction.   4. Racing – Fiction.   5. Dinosaurs – Fiction.]   I. Mark, Steve, ill.   II. Title
PZ.G82354Bu   1992
[E] – dc20   91-29649
                                                                                                            CIP
                                                                                                            AC

BUDDY ROCK'S RACE

Letting Go

Story by Kate Green
Illustrations by Steve Mark

I woke up early.
Today was the day
of the race at the Red Rock Games.
I had waited for weeks.
I'd practiced and trained,
run in the sun
and tramped through rain.
I was ready, steady,
primed, fine and fit!

Out the cave hole,
the dawn sky glowed.
Volcanos burned.
Black smoke churned
from a far peak.
None of that could stop
little dino-mite me!

I headed for the track
with my whole family.
They came to
cheer proud
and yell loud
in the big crowd.

"Go, Buddy Rocks!"
I heard them scream.
"Do your best!"

"First place!"
I shouted back.
"Nothing less!"

We lined up at the starting gate. I tied my sneakers with the swamp-green laces, then glanced (sort of scared) at my friends' faces. All eyes gleamed with the dream of First Prize.

There was Dennis Dimetrodon.
The fin on his back was slanted low-down for speed.
George Gorgosaurus was listless and fat.
He'd be no trouble, no question of that.
But next to him
was my biggest threat.
Sara and Cara,
the Triceratops twins
were planning a scheme:
how to cream the rest of us
and make a scam
out of our plan
to win.

"Get ready," a loud voice said.
I lowered my head.
The starting gun
blasted the sky.

I lifted my hefty foot
up high
and tripped over
Sara Triceratop's
thigh.

Down I rolled,
nose in the mud.
I landed with a giant thud,
square nowhere
at the starting gate.
There was no place to go
but *late,*
late,
late,
you loser.

The rest of the racers
stomped ahead
in a dead heat.
I crawled off the track
in defeat.

All that day
I couldn't talk.
Just walked over rocks
with my head hung down.
I hid in my room until night.
The moon sent silver light
through the cave cracks.
I wouldn't come out,
not even for my mother's
best swamp-grass pie.
"Baked just for you,"
she called,
"for giving it a super try."
But why, I thought,
Just why,
why,
why
did I fail?

There was a knock
at my rock.
In came my father.
We sat quietly for a while.
I was glad
he didn't make me smile
or cheer me up.
I was fed up with races
and wanted to forget
all traces of this day
forever.

Then in a voice
both loving and wise,
he gave me some dinosaur advice.
"Buddy Rocks," he rumbled,
"I know you stumbled
after training for a long time.
Your hopes were high
as a mountain.
And I know
you feel bad,
mad, lonely,
and ashamed.
You're
frustrated
that you
tripped
in the
tangling feet
and didn't
even get
to run in
the meet.

"I want you to know
that your feelings are true.
Something real about yourself
for you to know.
But there are times you have to let go
and accept something
you can not change.
The race is past.
You finished last.
But it's over, son.
And soon there will be
other races to run.
So what do you say?
Can you take a breath,
deep and slow,
and, when you breathe out,
let the thought of losing go?"

"I don't know," I said.
My voice was small
next to my tall father.
"I don't think I know
what letting go is.
It sounds like another way
of losing.
It sounds confusing to me."

"Picture this," he said,
"in the back of your mind."

"Do I have to?"
I heard myself whine.

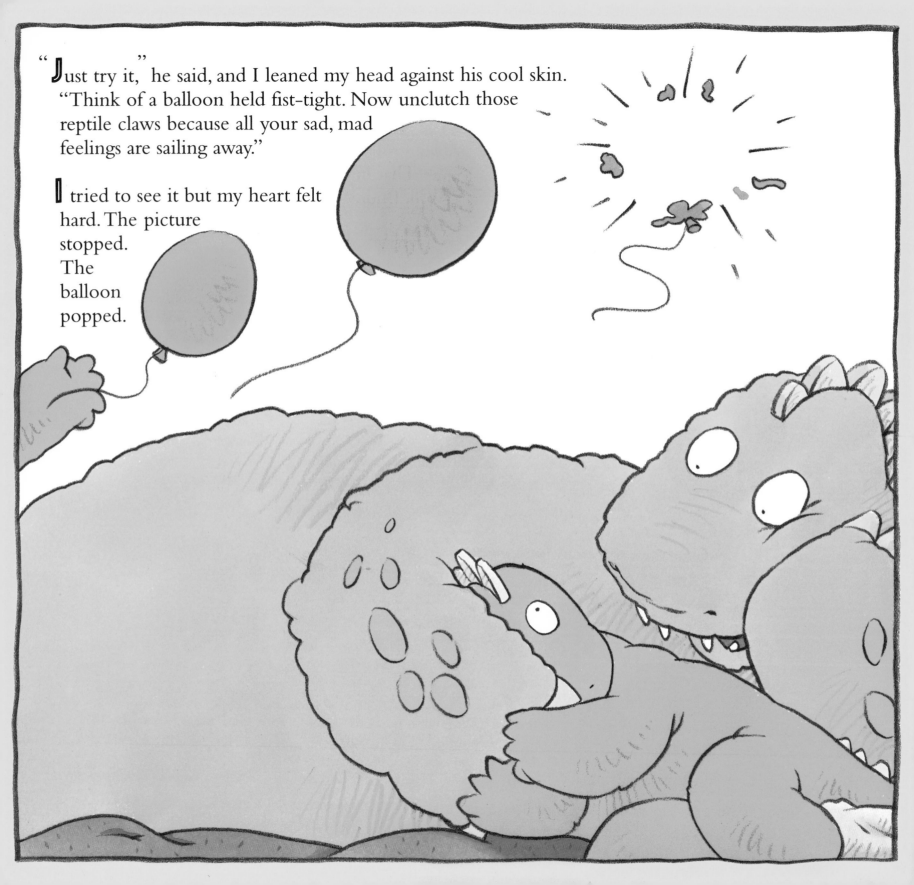

"Just try it," he said, and I leaned my head against his cool skin. "Think of a balloon held fist-tight. Now unclutch those reptile claws because all your sad, mad feelings are sailing away."

I tried to see it but my heart felt hard. The picture stopped. The balloon popped.

"Try this," he said, "with all that rage.
Think of it as a lion trapped in a cage.
Now unlock the door, swing it open wide.
See the lion run outside into the green freedom of space.
That lion is like your feeling of loss released.
Well, Buddy Rocks, do you feel more pleased?"

"Nope." I moped.
All I saw was a lion tryin'
to eat a dinosaur.

"Hmm," said Father.
"How about a fish?
The biggest fish
you could ever wish.
But instead of sticking him
on the stringer,
you want him to live!
So you unhook the lure
from the edge of his lip.
You let him go
slippery-sliding down
in the cool, black water.
That's how it feels
to let go of the pain
of something you
realize
you can't
change."

"I can't do it."
I knew I was pouting.
Soon, I worried,
he might start shouting at me.

"Let's try one more notion
of letting go.
Think of a trapeze.
You are swinging high
over the net
of all that would be
good to forget.
The next trapeze
is swinging back
for you to grab it.
But you have to let go
if you want to nab it
free and clear.

The circus crowd
lets out a cheer
as the Bravest Dinosaur
That Ever Was
lets go of one swing
to let a new thing
come toward him!"

I thought about that
and, just for a minute,
I thought I did it.
But then the sadness
grabbed hold of me again.
I scowled.

"It's okay,"
said that Dad of mine.
"You'll let go in your own good time
when you're able.
Now I'm going back to the table
for some of your mother's pie.
Bye," he said.

Then it came to me,
right to the core.
I felt like a giant tug of war.
I knew the race was done.
I hadn't won.
I hadn't even gotten to run.
And on one side
of that tugging rope
was *mad* and *mope*
and *yuck* and *nope*.

On the other end
of that rope
was *better next time*
and *cope* and *hope*
and *everybody makes mistakes*
and *try again*
and *you can do it!*

And what do you know?
All of a sudden
I did let go
just when I wasn't even trying.
I felt better then –
not even like crying,
but worn out anyway.

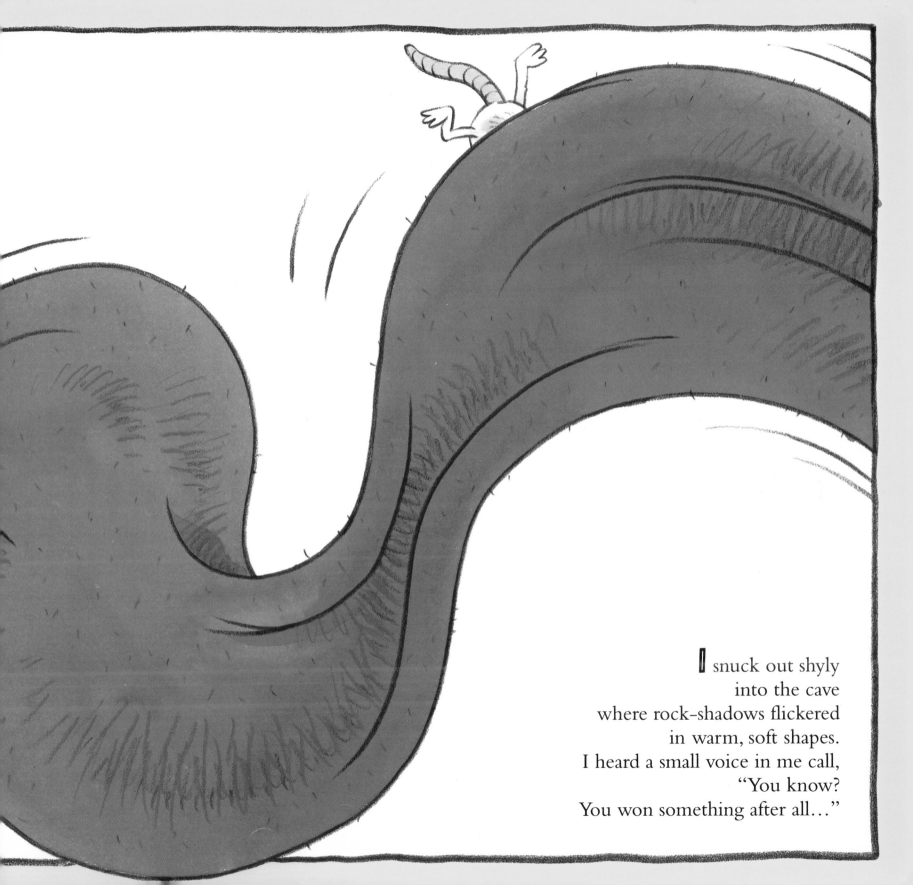

I snuck out shyly
into the cave
where rock-shadows flickered
in warm, soft shapes.
I heard a small voice in me call,
"You know?
You won something after all…"

Looking up
at the yellow moon,
I felt the pride inside
settle on my heart
like a big gold medal
full of light-shine.

"First Place
For Letting Go,"
said my heart-prize.
I closed my eyes
and smiled.